The Little Princess and The White Unicorn
Author: Claudine Darling
Illustrated by: Cimi Pham

This book is dedicated to one of the greatest gifts God ever gave me, Hope, Faith and Love

To: Americus and Tatum Adam, Ella Thompson, Analisa Clark, Oliva Clark – all of my little Great Nieces.

"Believing in yourself" when all odds are against you, is one of the greatest virtues one can ever hope to have.

Once upon a time, a little princess named Chloe lived in a beautiful castle upon a hill. She had pretty dresses, hats, jewelry and shoes. She also had a teacup, Maltese puppy named Pinky whom she adored that would follow her everywhere she went.

But her heart longed to see a White Unicorn. Every morning, Chloe would get out of bed and sit down in front of her mirror. She would brush her hair and ask, "Mirror, mirror, can you please tell me when I will see a White Unicorn?"

The mirror knew that this wish would never come true. The mirror
replied back to her, laughing aloud. "Little Princess, Chloe, you will
see a White Unicorn, when you have seen a White Lion."

Chloe opened her White Unicorn jewelry box and watched the
White Unicorn spinning around and around listening to the pretty
music playing chimes. She sat in her chair for several minutes
dreaming about seeing a White Unicorn.

She then turned around in her chair and stared at all the White Unicorn pictures she had drawn every day on all her walls. She looked at her art table with all the White Unicorns that she had made with her play-dough. Chloe felt sad. In her heart, she really wanted to see a White Unicorn.

Pinky started jumping up and down, barking. Chloe looked at Pinky barking and suddenly got up in a hurry. She closed her White Unicorn jewelry box and looked in the mirror and said with a loud voice. "Okay mirror, mirror! Then I shall look for a White Lion! I will look and I will look! I shall see a White Lion! I will! I will! I will see a White Unicorn!"

She quickly got dressed in her favorite pink dress and put on her
sparkling pink shoes. She opened her jewelry box that had the White
Unicorn that twirled and sang. While listening to the Unicorn sing,
she put on her Unicorn earrings, her Unicorn bracelet, her Unicorn
necklace and her Unicorn headband.

She then raced downstairs, out the door to the flower garden. Pinky, all along, running fast behind her. "Come on Pinky!" she said, as she walked, hurriedly, around the garden saying, "We are going to see a White Lion today!"

The garden was filled with beautiful flowers. As Chloe walked
around the garden, with Pinky behind her, she saw a mother bunny
and her babies. She ran up to the mother bunny and asked, "Hello
Ms. Bunny! "Have you seen a White Lion?" The mother bunny
looked at her with wide eyes, shook its head and said, "No, I have
not seen a White Lion." She quickly gathered her baby bunnies and
happily hopped away.

"Oh my," Chloe said. She looked around and saw a path leading to
a forest. She and Pinky started running down the forest path
together. She saw a Chipmunk up in the tree and asked, "Mr.
Chipmunk, have you seen a White Lion?" The Chipmunk quickly
gathered his nuts around him and said, "No, I have not seen a
White Lion and hurried into his tree den."

Chloe and Pinky walked along the forest path. Pinky was sniffing all
the bushes along the way. They finally came to a pond and a fish
jumped up in the air. Chloe asked. "Have you seen a White Lion?"
The fish answered her, "No I have not seen a White Lion," and dived
back into the pond and swam away.

Then, Chloe asked a frog and he said, "No, I have not seen a White Lion." And then she asked a red bird and the red bird said, "No, I have not seen a White Lion." And then she asked a raccoon, and raccoon said, "No, I have not seen a White Lion."

As Chloe and Pinky walked further along the path, she asked a fox, "Have you seen a White Lion?" And the fox said, "No, I have not seen a White Lion." And then she asked a turtle, and then she asked a porcupine and finally, she asked a deer. And they all said, "No, I have not seen a White Lion."

It was starting to get dark. Chloe was getting tired. She was hoping she would see a White Lion so she could see a White Unicorn. Chloe picked up Pinky and held her close, petting her softly. She then sat down and started to cry. She really wanted to see a White Lion so she could see a White Unicorn.

While her tears fell, a bright light appeared in the sky and silver shining stars appeared. She looked up and there on a high rock, above her, was a White Lion. Pinky jumped out of her arms and started barking, loudly.

She quickly stood up, grabbed Pinky in her arms and looked at the White Lion. He was a large White Lion with big green eyes. The White Lion looked at her closely and asked, "Why are you crying Little Princess, Chloe?"

Chloe stepped back and asked softly. "How do you know my name?"
The White Lion with a loud roar, laughed out-loud and said, "I am
King of the forest. I know everyone's name in the forest, my dear."

Chloe wiped her tears away, while looking at the White Lion with
big green eyes and said. "I am crying because my mirror at home
told me I needed to see a White Lion, so I could see a White Unicorn."

I asked the animals in the forest and they all said, "No, they have not
seen a White Lion." "But here you are," Chloe said, softly. The
White Lion jumped down from the rock and stood in front of Chloe.
Still holding and petting Pinky, Chloe slowly backed away.

All of a sudden, all the animals that Chloe spoke to came out from behind the forest trees and sat around the White Lion. The White Lion began to speak again. "Dear, my dear, Little Princess, Chloe. I am the White Lion you have been looking for. I am here. And, you, my dear Little Princess Chloe have seen me."

The little animals sitting around them started smiling and clapping. "My little friends here told you, "No they have not seen a White Lion," because I watch over them here in the forest and they do not want anyone to come hurt them nor hurt me."

The White Lion looked at Chloe closely, in silence, and then began to speak again. "Okay, then, Little Princess Chloe, I want you to do as I say and I will grant your wish to see a White Unicorn."

The White Lion closed his big green eyes and said. "I want you to close your eyes and turn around in a circle and pet your dog, Pinky, and say out loud." "I love my Daddy! I love my Mommy! I love my sister! I love my brother! I love my home! And, I want to see a White Unicorn!"

Chloe closed her eyes and said all the words the White Lion had
wanted her to say. A wind began to blow and the trees started to
shake and all the little animals ran behind the trees. Chloe held Pinky
tight against her. She began to feel dizzy. She could hear the White
Lion roaring. All she knew is she wanted to go home.

The wind stopped. Chloe opened her eyes. She was at home, sitting in front of her mirror in her pink dress, holding Pinky in her lap.

Chloe looked in the mirror and said. "Mirror, mirror, you told me if I saw a White Lion, you would grant me my wish to see a White Unicorn!" The mirror started shaking. "So I did say that! And, you did see a White Lion Little Princess, Chloe. So, you did!"

The shaking mirror then showed Chloe a White Lion on a rock with shining silver stars behind it. And the White Lion in the mirror roared and said aloud to Chloe, "Go and look out your window!"

Chloe ran to the window with Pinky wagging her tail, jumping up and down behind her barking. She looked out the window into the flower garden and there she saw a beautiful White Unicorn. It had braided sparkling colored hair, a colored tail and colored pink nails with a Unicorn colored headband with flowers and sparking blue eyes. There was a brightly colored rainbow behind the White Unicorn.

Chloe danced around her room with Pinky, smiling and waving at the sparkling White Unicorn who kicked up its white legs as if to wave back at Chloe. She and Pinky watched the White Unicorn dance around the garden for a long time. Chloe was so happy. She wanted this moment to last forever.

She ran over to her jewelry box and opened it. The White Unicorn on top started twirling around and around, playing music. The White Unicorns she made on her art table began to dance. All of the White Unicorn pictures on her walls began to sparkle with glitter. Her bedroom with all her beautiful White Unicorns began to sing, dance and shine with glitter.

Chloe stood at the window for a long time watching the beautiful White Unicorn. Then it began to get dark outside and she started to feel tired. With sleepy eyes, she waved good-bye to the White Unicorn who bowed its head to Chloe and slowly walked into the forest and disappeared. She turned around with sleepy eyes, yawned and smiled. There was Pinky fast asleep on her bed.

Chloe laid down in her bed. She closed her eyes and remembered what the White Lion had said to her. Then she whispered, softly. "I love my Mommy! I love my Daddy! I love my sister! I love my brother! I love my home! And, I want to see a White Unicorn!"

Each and every night when Chloe went to sleep, she whispered the White Lion's words. And then, a beautiful White Unicorn would appear in her dreams.

THE END